A RUMPUS OF Rhymes

A Book of Noisy Poems

BOBBI KATZ

illustrated by
SUSAN ESTELLE KWAS

Dutton Children's Books ◎ New York

All poems are published with the permission of the author.
The following poems were published previously: "Parade" copyright © 1994
by Bobbi Katz; "Advice from Aunt Prudence"
and "Summer Jazz" copyright © 1995 by Bobbi Katz

Library of Congress Cataloging-in-Publication Data

Katz, Bobbi.
A rumpus of rhymes: a book of noisy poems/
by Bobbi Katz; illustrated by Susan Estelle Kwas.—
1st American ed.   p.cm.
ISBN 0-525-46718-1
1. Noise—Juvenile poetry. 2. Sound—Juvenile poetry.
3. Sounds—Juvenile poetry. 4. Children's poetry, American.
[1. Noise—Poetry. 2. Sound—Poetry. 3. American poetry.]
I. Kwas, Susan Estelle, ill. II. Title.
PS3561.A7518 R86 2001
811'.54—dc21   00-065786

Published in the United States 2001 by Dutton Children's Books,
a division of Penguin Putnam Books for Young Readers
345 Hudson Street, New York, New York 10014
www.penguinputnam.com

Designed by Sara Reynolds and Richard Amari
Printed in Hong Kong
First Edition
1 2 3 4 5 6 7 8 9 10

For Barry and Wendy, with applause!
B.K.

For my parents, Al and Jackie, for putting up with all my noise!
S.E.K.

LISTEN

Libraries have signs like these:

QUIET **DON'T TALK**

SILENCE PLEASE

By day they're read by me and you.
Mostly we do what the signs tell us to.
Now imagine the library late at night.
The windows are shut and the door's
  locked tight.
But the words in the books are wide awake,
and the noisy words start to itch and ache!
They've been sitting in silence
  on printed pages,
not making a sound for ages and ages.

Suddenly they can't bear the quiet.
They burst out of the books
  in a rackety riot!
Splash and splatter—

BANG
BOP
BOOM!

Words bounce and scramble
  through the room.

s p i t t e r   s p u t t e r

CLANK

CLUNK
CRASH

buzz **BANG** thunder

splish
splosh
splash

Once words begin to peep and **POP**,
it's clear that they can never stop.
Words that ***swizzle,***
s n o r e,
and SNEEZE
cannot return to

SILENCE PLEASE

Since noisy words now need new homes,
let them all move into poems!
Poems to sing or read aloud.
Poems that *like* a noisy crowd.

Imagine the library late at night—
and a riot of words.
Could it happen? It might.
LISTEN!

BUMPTIOUS BURPS

We have a knack for sneak attacks.
We always show off best
at churches during silent prayer,
at schools when there's a test.
We like to choose a public place,
where there's a quiet crowd....
Then when we

gra-graah-
graah-
graah
greps

we sound
especially
loud!

ADVICE FROM AUNT PRUDENCE

While sipping soda, never *guzzle.*
While spooning noodles, never **slurp.**
Unless you're in Japan,
where I understand you can.

HECTOR McVECTOR

Hector McVector, the hiccup collector,
has tapes and a tiny recorder.
Wherever a hiccup gets **Hicc-UPPED**
he's there,
in order to tape the disorder.

BUBBLE GUM

Chunk-a-hunk-a bubble gum.
Chunk-a-hunk-a chew.
Chonk the chunk into a hunk
    of squishy, squoshy goo!
Snap it and then **C R A C K** it.
Now your tongue knows what to do:
Lob the glob inside your lips
and push the whole thing through!
Now you've got a bubble.
It's getting bigger....
S T O P !
Chunk-a-hunk-a bubble gum
Chunk-a-hunk-a...

POP!

CRUDITÉS

CHINKETY-CHONKETY
Carrots and celery
CHIPPETY-CHOPPETY-NICKETY-KNOCK
CHINKETY-CHONKETY
Carrots and celery
dance to the knife
on the chopping block.
CHINKETY-CHONKETY-CHUNKETY-CHIP
Open your mouth
and in they'll skip.

CAUGHT IN THE ACT

"Hands off those potato chips.
I'm saving them to serve with dips!"

But those crispy chips peered out at me.
"Your mom won't notice two or three."

And now I'm grounded! What a pain—
betrayed by *crinkling* cellophane!

HAY FEVER SEASON

Spring is the season
for sna-sna-sna-
SNEEZING.

Sniff-sniff-sniff-sniffle
kERRrCHoo!
When daffodils blossom,
and birds build their nests,
I get to do my thing, too!

kERRrCHoo!

RAIN DANCE

When I wear my yellow slicker
with its matching yellow hat,
I can tune into the tap dance
of the raindrops' **pitter pat.**
I can listen to their time steps
tap out rhythms as they land.
I'm a walking music station
with my private tap-dance band!

SPRING CONVERSATIONS

"**Whisk!**"
whirls the jump rope,
twirling
around.

"**THUD!**"

say the sneakers,
bouncing off the ground.

"**SMACK!**"

says the ball to the catcher's mitt.

"**WHACK!**"

says the bat when it makes a hit.

When somebody tosses
a handful of jacks,
there's a cascading ripple
of clickety clacks.
"**THUMPITY, THUMP, THUMP!**"
echoes the concrete
as the basketball
travels
down
the court
across the street.

WILLIS WALKER, NONSTOP TALKER

Jibber-jab-jibber
chit-chat-yak-yak...
When Willis starts talking,
who can talk back?

LYDIA LUCE

Lydia Luce prefers pits to pure juice,
especially the pits of the prune.
Her teeth **CLONK-A-CLONK** them
like castanets,
while she tangoes in time to their tune.

SUMMER JAZZ

Katydids fiddling with the crickets!
The caterpillar's selling tickets.
Rum-strum bullfrogs playing bass.
Jiving spiders spinning lace.
Bebop beetles boogie to the beat.
Even daddy longlegs tap their feet.
Mosquitoes buzz and go right to it.

Walking sticks strut.
     My, how they do it!
The night gets hotter.
     The band plays louder.
The man in the moon
     takes a headache powder.
The praying mantis says, "Amen!
Tomorrow night let's jam again!"

HIS WIFE SAID...

The next time, Noah, I insist,

when we have guests, I'll make the list!

The rowdy crowd that you invite

creates a rumpus day and night.

With **honk**ing geese and **bleat**ing sheep,

I can only dream of sleep!

My temper's growing very short.

The hippos and the rhinos **SNORT.**

The baboons **bellow.**

The beavers **thump.**

The raccoons *yoddle.*

The kangas jump.

The monkeys **SHRIEK.**

The lions **ROAR.**

And in the din I hear you...

s n o r e !

THE STREET
WHERE NO ONE SLEEPS

Lucía's forced to wear ear stoppers
due to double-parking coppers.
When grumpy drivers cannot pass,
they lean upon their horns, alas!

TOOT, TOOT, TOOTS
     and
BEEP, BEEP, BEEPS

guarantee that no one sleeps.

PARADE

On the Fourth of July, oh isn't it grand,
when d'Agostino's Memorial Band
goes marching by **Padoom! Padum!**
filling the town with the boom
    of a drum?
Brass trumpets flashing in the sun
play a march and everyone
is tapping his feet or clapping his hands.
On the Fourth of July, oh isn't it grand?

The mayor rides by in an open car.
Then come the Daughters of Eastern Star.
Police Chief Tripoli **klip-klops** on a horse
with three mounted riders,
    the town police force.
The fire trucks go rolling by,
and Clan MacLeod with heads held high—
their tartan kilts above their knees—
pipe ancient Scottish melodies.

Next, majorettes twirl silver sticks,
and the Continentals of '76
With a RAP of a drum
and a toot of a fife
bring Washington's army back to life.
And suddenly I understand
the Fourth of July!
Oh, isn't it grand?

MUMBO-JUMBO BREAKFAST

Mumbo-jumbo breakfast
is the meal that talks the most,
from the *sizzle* of the bacon
to the **munchy crunchy** toast.
First the kettle starts to whistle.
There goes Baby's bowl—**KERPLOP!**
Now she grabs her spoon and bangs it,
and she doesn't want to stop.
Glasses clink and dishes rattle.
Pots and pans go CLITTER CLATTER.
Pour some milk on your rice crispies
and they'll start to chitter chatter
while the coffee percolator
keeps repeating **blup-blup-blup.**
That's the coffee's way of saying,
"Someone, pour me in a cup!"

Mumbo-jumbo breakfast
is a noisy morning diet,
when the folded paper napkin
is the only thing that's quiet.

SCHOOL BUS RAP

I'm a bin, bin, bin.
I'm a
be, bee, beep.
I'm a bus.
A school bus.

MUFF, MUFF, CHUFF!
My motor's rough.
My hard seats squeak.
My gears say **eeek!**
Rain or snow,
I just go, go, go.
I don't fuss.
I'm a bus.

Instead of saying,
"Slow down, please,"
a strong foot gives my brakes a squeeze.
I **wheeze** and **wheeze** and
wheeze and **wheeze!**
I can't forget
I'm not a jet.
I'm a bus—**chuff!**
A school bus.

"Hey there, you kid."
Toot, toot, toot!
"Take a seat.
You're on my route."

I'm a bus—**chuff!**
A school bus—**chuff!**
A school bus...

THE WITCH'S INVITATION

Ga-bumba-bumba-bumba,
won't you come along with me
to the monsters' midnight jamboree?
You can cackle with my sisters
and try on their pointy hats
while their cats are *hiss-a-hissing*
at the *flap-pa-dap-pa* bats.

The mummy cases open
with a **CRICKY-CRACKY-C R E A K.**
The mummies thump across the floor.
(Of course, they never speak.)
You'll meet every kind of monster
at the monsters' jamboree!
Ga-bumba-bumba-bumba,
won't you come along with me?

The skeletons are dancing:
CLICK-A-TICKA-TICKA-TACK.
First they clap their bones together.
Then they swing-a-ding them back.
Glippy gloppy goblins grunt,
"Grunch-a-grinch-a-gru!"
which is just their way of saying
that they'd like some lizard stew.

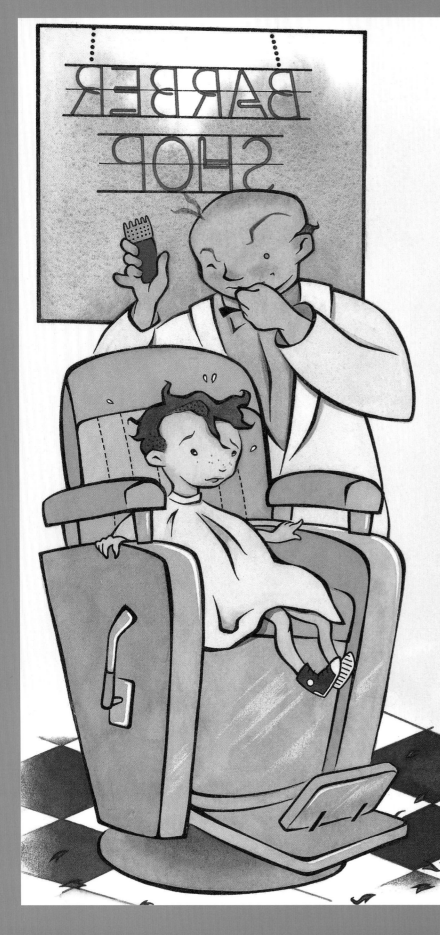

AT THE BARBERSHOP

Draped in a cape—
a towel beneath my chin.
Snip-Snip!
Clip-Clip!
Scissors begin.
Zizzz goes the razor.
Hair slips to the floor.
"Scuffle-duffle!" says the broom.
"Ding-dong!" says the door.
"When," asks a man,
"can you cut my hair?"
"When I'm finished,"
    says the barber,
"with this kid in the chair.
And that (**Snip-Snip**)
will be a short wait.
Just a touch
        of the razor
            will make
                both sides straight."

He turned on the razor.

Z a - z a - z z z i z z .

"O O P S!" said the barber.

"Golly! Gee whiz!

The razor shaved a little wide.

I'll even off the other side."

But…

    the razor

took a buzzing ride

when it *za-za-zizzzed* the other side.

Hair flew in the air,

        then fell to the floor.

The man

  who'd wanted

    a haircut before

      slipped back out

        the ding-dong door.

The barber smiled.

"Don't worry, son.

You'll look handsome

when I'm done."

He picked up the scissors…

B r r i n g

    went the phone.

The barber went to get it.

I was alone.

    Off with the towel.

      Off with the cape.

        Down with my money.

          It's time to escape!!

WASHING MACHINE

I'm the washing machine.
I make dirty clothes clean
so that nobody has to rub:
**Glubita glubita
glubita
glubita glubita
glubita...
GLUB.**
*Swizzle-dee-swash
Swizzle-dee-swash*
I talk to myself,
while I do the wash!
Babba-da-swaba
I change my song,
as the cycle moves along.
Soapsuds gurgle through my hose.

Then...
Blub-blub-a-dubba
I rinse the clothes.
**Blippety-blop
blippety-blop**
I *spin spin spin*
and then...
I stop.

PIGGY BANK

Money, money—yum-yum-yummy!
Drop some in my nice fat tummy!
TCHUNK! clunks a quarter.
CLING! dings a dime.
My tummy sings at feeding time.

AN UNUSUAL SHEPHERD

Not every shepherd shepherds sheep
that **bah-bah-bah** or bleat-**bleat**-b l e a t.
Phineas Knox herds flocks of clocks.
No wool have they—just *ticks* and *tocks.*

THE WIND

I am the wind of spring,
flap-snapping the laundry
and ripping off a shirt.
Hold tight to your kite
the day I come to play!
Feel me in your hand—
tugging-tugging.
I am the magician.
ABRACADABRA!
See the daffodils bend
and hear them rustle
at my command.

I am the wind of summer.
The welcome wind.
Gently swooshing
against your hot cheeks
at the playground
and twirling your pinwheel.
I woof the sailboats across the water
and cool the sweaty players
on the baseball fields.
 Doze on a hammock—
 I'll be gently swooshing through your
dreams...
Swooooosh... Swooooosh...

I am the wind the witches ride,
the wind of fall.
When you trick-or-treat,
crunching leaves beneath your feet,
then I'll go haunting, too—
rattling the windows
when you knock on the door,
crackling bare branches of the trees,
hissing at the jack-o'-lantern's candle.
HISSSS!

I am the wind of winter.
Whip! Wallop! Whoosh!
Bundle up, when you hear me huffle.
I'll nip your nose.
I'll bite your toes.
I blow the snow
and I'll blow you, too!
Whip! Wallop! Whoosh!

SEA SPEAK

If every ocean
and every sea
held an intercoastal
spelling bee,
with all the surf
from far and near,
these are some
of the words we'd hear:

thundering

WHACKING

SMACKING

SPLASHING

lashing

SLAPPING

lapping

Licking

TICKLING

gurgling

spurting

spritzing

POUNDING...

and the sound
of that oh-so-gentle inhalation:

frooooosh!

THUNDER

Hear him **tumble**
    grumble,
        rumble...
BASH, CRASH, BLUNDER—

      old grouch thunder!
Always in a mood to fight,
morning, afternoon, or night.
Lightning quickly answers back
with a zigzag
      flashing

CRACK!

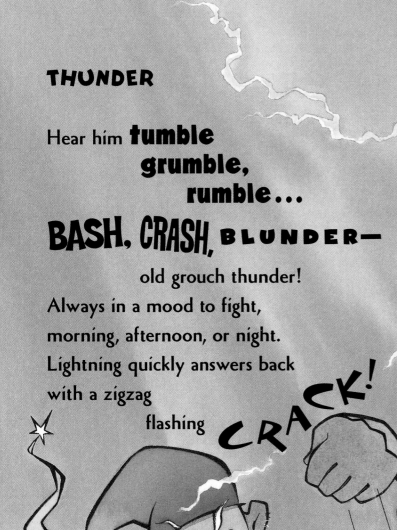

WE'RE CROWS

TWEET! TWEET!
    Chirp! Chirp!
        Trill-a-trill-a-trill!
Birds that please have songs like these.
Our call is raw and shrill.
    ## CAW! CAW! CAW!
        We're crows!

When the Birding Club goes stalking,
they whisper in awed hushes
if they spot some crummy plovers,
yellow finches, or gray thrushes.
But they don't get excited
when our flying flocks are sighted.
    ## CAW! CAW! CAW!
        We're crows!

People put seeds in bird feeders,
then they twitter with great glee
over every rotten robin,
every black-capped chickadee.
But do people try to lure us?
At the best, they just endure us.
Foolish farmers cannot bear us,
but their straw men do not scare us.
    ## CAW! CAW! CAW!
        We're crows!

No one ever tries to count us
because we are *everywhere—*
roosting on the treetops—
        swooping through the air.
We're not likely to be found
on the Endangered Species List,
but if we were to disappear,
we think we might be missed.
No ## CAW! CAW! CAW!

    No crows!

SNOW SCENE

In the hush of the cold
    of a winter's night,
snowflakes layer the town in white.
    Layers and layers
of white eiderdown
    softly envelop the sleeping town,
bundling houses
    and blanketing trees,
      feathering hills
        to be
          cushions
            for skis,
changing the shapes
    and blurring the edges
of automobiles
    and window ledges,

filling the night
(who would deny it?)
with a magical sound—
a particular quiet.
LISTEN!